THE FEARLESS ADVENTURERS

AMRUTHA.G

Contents

THE BRAVE TRIO

PART 1 and PART 2

THE BRAVE TRIO (PART 1)

Once upon a time, there lived three girls. One morning the family sat together to eat breakfast. This was not just any morning; it was the morning of the first day of their summer vacation.

"Mom, it is raining so heavily outside; it's the first day of vacation! I thought I could play outside after breakfast," said Rose while looking out the window. Rose and Lily were the mature ones. Tina was extremely creative but a bit childish. "Yes, it has been pouring since last night. I hope there won't be a flood or anything like that," said Mom. Simultaneously, Dad turned on the news. The news had a flash warning of an upcoming flood. "Oh no! We have a very high risk of a flood! I think it's better if we move to someplace higher," said Dad. "What?! Just temporarily, right?" asked Tina. "Yes, why don't we go to my sister's house? Her house is a three-story building," suggested Mom. "Hmm, okay, kids, pack your bags. We need to leave soon," said Dad. So, all of them packed the necessities and went to Ms Bright's house.

"Welcome! I thought of inviting you since I too have seen the news but look at you! Here already!" said Aunt Bright with a laugh. "Oh, hello there, who are you!" asked Lily while looking at the cat. "She is my pet cat, Luna. She also has a kitten named Bella," said Aunt Bright. "I didn't know that!" said Rose, who is always mesmerized by seeing cats. "Aren't you the cutest kitty in the world, Bella?" said Lily. "No, dogs are better," said Tina, the dog lover of the family

Time flew by. The next day came to action. "I'm just so bored. I have nothing to do!" said Tina. "Me too, my best friend is so busy that she can't even call!" said Rose. "At least you have a best friend! I have no one," said Lily. "Don't say that! We are your best friends," said Tina. "Meow! Meow!" said Bella the kitten. "Look! Bella's so funny! It's like she is trying to talk to us!" said Rose. "Come here, Bella! I have milk for you!" said Aunt Bright. "Meow?" said Luna as if she was asking for food. "Don't worry, Luna! I will never forget you." Assured Aunt Bright as she was giving Luna milk. "I'm going to draw something. It's too boring," said Tina. Dad was watching the news, and it showed people getting rescued in boats. "Thank goodness we are not the people getting rescued!" said Rose. "But I've always wanted to go on a boat ride. How cool would it feel! The cold breeze and the feeling of floating on water are like denying gravity!" said Lily. "No way! I hate boats! What if the boat turned over and we sank? Or what if some shark bites our boat? Or what if—" As Tina was talking anxiously, Rose interrupted and said, "That's enough, Tina! we get the picture!" "Yeah, Tina, riding boats is not that scary," said Lily.

Rose asked her mom, "What is for lunch? I'm so hungry." "It's not even twelve, and you're asking for lunch already?" asked Mom. Rose giggled. "But we are hungry, Mom! Can you please make pancakes or all of us?" asked Lily. "Fine, it will be ready soon," said Mom.

After lunch, Aunt Bright went to take a short nap. Dad turned on the news as usual. "What is so important in the news? Only videos of people getting rescued are shown there!" asked Lily, "Yeah, but I'm going to watch it anyway," answered Dad. "I will watch the news with you, Dad. I have nothing to do anyway," said Tina. An hour passed by; nothing had changed. It was still raining, and Dad was still watching the news.

Tina said, "I'll quit watching the news. Too boring!" said Tina. "Your loss!" said Dad. "I want to swim in the flood water," said Tina. "What has gotten to your mind? Don't you know the dangers of flood water!" said Rose. "No," answered Tina. "Well, Tina, there is a high risk of you getting an electric shock. As the electric wires fall into the water, water, as a very good conductor, will give you a shock," explained Lily.

"Anyways, does anyone know what day it is tomorrow?" asked Lily. "Yeah, it's Sunda – oh wait a minute! It's your 13th birthday!" exclaimed Rose. "Yup, an official teenager!" shouted Lily. "Isn't it funny all our birthdays are so near to each other?" asked Rose. "It sure is!" said Lily. "My birthday is coming in a few days too!" said Rose. "Not just any birthday, your 14th birthday! Advance wishes to you!" said Lily. "Same to you!" said Rose.

"My birthday too comes soon! It's so exciting!" said Tina. "Oh! How did I forget your 12th birthday?!" said Lily. "Well, I guess advance wishes to you too! Since there's barely a week for your birthday!" said Rose.

Everything was going well. "Tina, don't shake the table," said Rose. "I'm not!" said Tina. "Then who's shaking it?" asked Lily. "No one! Girls, it's an earthquake! Quick! Everyone, get to safety!" shouted Dad. "CRASH!" The chandelier fell and broke into pieces. Tina let out a blood-curdling scream. The earthquake made everything fall off the shelves. "Oh my! There is an earthquake!" shouted Aunt Bright, who woke up hearing all the noise.

"Quick, Dad! Turn on the radio! Who knows what will happen!" shouted Rose. "I don't have the radio in my pocket! It's somewhere on the shelf," replied Dad. "Ah! Everyone! Hide under a table, bed, or something," shouted Mom.

Everyone hid under the furniture. The cats hid under the bed with Aunt Bright. All of them heard the crashing noises of the trees and prayed that they would be safe. "These were the worst five minutes of my life!" shouted Rose after the earthquake stopped. Lily and Tina nodded their heads, agreeing with Rose.

Because of their quick response to the earthquake, no one got hurt. The house was a bit messed up, almost everything in shelves or cupboards fell on the floor. The family was in shock as they were not in an earthquake-prone area. Aunt had a mini heart attack due to this sudden shaking. The kids were scared but recovered soon because this was a thrilling experience for them. The cats were shivering in fear.

"Okay, this is too much. I'm going to sit under the table and read my favorite book," said Lily. As she was reading, she asked her sisters, "What if we also pack emergency bags? Like with food, clothes, water, etc? won't it be so fun?" "What a great idea! Let's ask our mom," said Rose.

"Mom, can we pack our backpacks?" asked Rose. "Why? Where are you going to go?" asked Mom. "Nowhere, just for fun. Please?" asked Rose. "What are you going to pack?" asked Mom. "Just some food, water, clothes, etc. Can we please do it?" begged Lily. "To waste our supplies? No," replied Mom

"Let them have their fun; it's not like they have anything else to do anyways in this flood," Dad said to Mom. "Fine, pack whatever you want," said Mom. "Yay!" Squealed Rose and Lily with excitement. "Tina, wake up sleepyhead! We are going to pack our emergency bags! Don't you want to join?" said Rose. "What! Wait for me!" said Tina, who had just gotten up.

So, as mentioned above, they packed their bags. Rose packed her bag with food materials like instant soup, instant noodles, breakfast cereals, etc. She also packed a solar-powered stove, a flashlight, a box full of batteries, walkie-talkies, a toolbox, a phone, and some energy drinks.

Lily packed her bag with board games. She also packed her bag with a huge foldable tent with four partitions. She packed her bag with almost the same food items as Rose.

She packed some instant ready-to-eat snacks, too.

Tina packed her bag with ropes, cat food, two gallons of water, her journal, sketchbook, a change of clothes, sleeping bags, etc. Mom said, "Those are a lot of things; I think it's better if you unpack them." "No way!" the three kids shouted. "Come on, let them do as they wish! If we need anything, we can ask them," said Dad. "Okay, if you say so," said Mom

"We packed for ourselves, but we didn't pack for you! Come on, girls, get me Mom's largest handbag! We will pack another emergency bag," said Rose. Tina got her mom's largest handbag, and the three started to pack it with all the essentials, like some snacks, water, utensils, and blankets.

"Wow! I'm surprised that you could fit so many things in that small bag!" said Aunt Bright. "Kids, I have good news! The weather forecast has informed me that there is a very low to no chance of getting another earthquake," said Dad. "If you are trying to convince us to unpack our bag, then better change your mind! Cause we are not changing ours!" said Lily. "Don't talk like that!" said Mom. "Let them have their fun. When we were kids, we used to do all sorts of silly things like this," said Aunt Bright. Dad called emergency services to clean up the mess caused by the fallen chandelier. Thankfully, everyone was safe even after the earthquake.

"Oh, I almost forgot to pack my forest guide!" exclaimed Rose. "Girls, I have this radio that can read out the news; if you want to pack it, I'll happily give it to you," said Aunt Bright. "Oh wow, thanks, Aunty! We would love to have this in our bags!" said Rose. "How should we turn it on?" asked Tina. "You just need to press that red button to switch it on; if you want to change channels long, press that same button," said Aunt Bright. "Thank you so much, Aunty. This might be very useful for us," said Lily.

It was eight at night, and the family was sitting down for dinner when suddenly, they heard a huge noise! They were scared for life! The house broke into two! All were in a panic, even though the news said that there was a very low chance of an earthquake, it happened! Everyone hid under the dining table. All of them managed to drop to the floor, cover their heads and necks, and hold on to a shelter till the earthquake ended. After the earthquake, everyone was in a panic.

"Oh my! This earthquake is an example of how a few minutes of change can make a big impact!" It barely lasted for a few minutes but broke the house into two!" said Mom. Thankfully, no one was hurt. But the house was severely damaged. "This earthquake was due to the increased mining activity near this area," said Dad. "What do we do?!" asked Tina. "I'll just call the disaster management and inform them," said Dad. Mom took photos of the damage, and Aunt Bright was checking the house for any gas leaks, electrical lines, and water lines for damage.

"FIRE! FIRE!" shouted Tina. "Where?!" shouted Dad. "Near this electrical cable!" shouted Tina. "We must evacuate immediately!" said Aunt Bright. Now, Mom called the fire station, and the kids were ready with their bags. "Good thing we packed our bags earlier!" said Lily. Dad rushed to get important documents like birth certificate, driving license, etc.

Everyone packed whatever they could find and rushed out of the house. Since there was a flood, the disaster management arrived in two boats. "Let's check if everyone here is safe," said Dad. "Luna! We forgot Luna! She is still in the house!" shouted Lily. The firefighters went inside to get Luna. They told them to get on the boats. The family bid goodbye to their home as it was now completely ruined.

All of them climbed inside the boats, which were tied with rope to the broken building. But to everyone's horror, the ropes somehow got cut! Fortunately, the parents' boat was saved as the disaster management came back just in time with Luna, but the kids and Bella the kitten went floating somewhere in their boats!

All the kids screamed helplessly. No one was able to help them!

"HELP! HELP!" The girls cried. "Maybe everything is over, maybe this is the end!" said Tina. "Are you crazy?! Never lose hope! We still have our bags with us and Bella to support us!" shouted Rose.

Rose and Lily desperately tried to row the boat, but they didn't know how to. "I can't make the boat go that way!" shouted Rose. Tina fainted due to the shock. Rose and Lily gave up trying to row the boat as it was no use. After a long time, Tina woke up. "Was the boat a dream?" asked Tina. After looking around, Tina came to know that it was indeed not a dream. "Where on earth are we?!"

shouted Tina. "We don't know either! Just try to sleep now; we will go wherever the boat takes us," replied Rose.

"Yes, Tina, calm down. Maybe when we wake up, we will crash onto our beach or at least be rescued somehow," said Lily. Everyone, including the cat, slept on the boat, hoping that they would be rescued the next day. Then, they all heard an unexpected noise. The boat had crashed on an island. "I suppose we were drifting in our city, then drifted into a river then an ocean or sea, and we got crashed into an island," said Lily. "I guess so," replied Rose.

The sun Rose, so the girls knew that it was daytime. "Why don't we go and check out this island? It's not like we have anything else to do now anyway," said Tina. "Okay! Come on, girls, let's tie our boat to this tree and then explore this island," said Rose. "What do we tie our boat with? We don't have any ropes!" said Lily. "Hmm yeah, good point... I have an idea: all of you stay here on the boat. Lily, please look after Bella and Tina, look after all our bags. I will go and check if there is anything to tie our boat with," said Rose.

So, Rose went in search of something strong to tie the boat. She came back within a minute and asked Tina for gloves. Luckily, they had a pair of rubber gloves and also a strong pair of scissors. Rose wore the gloves and took the scissors. Then she called Lily for help. Lily told Tina to look after everything and went to help Rose.

With Lily's help, Rose cut a creeper with scissors and brought it back to the boat to use as a rope. "Wow! How did you find such a strong plant!" exclaimed Tina. "Well, I was walking, and then something made me trip over. I looked down to see this creeper and thought that it would be perfect to tie our boat," said Rose. "Then she called me to help while cutting this creeper. Gosh, it was so hard to cut!" said Lily

So, they tied the boat, and everyone got out of it. Then, it started to drizzle. As most cats don't like water, Bella meowed so loudly that everyone shut their ears. "What do we do now? We can't sleep in the rain!" said Tina. "Rose, isn't that a small cave there?" asked Lily. "I think so! Let's go and have a look," said Rose. "That's kind of risky... but we have no choice!" said Tina. So, everyone went inside the cave with their bags, including Bella.

"I just realized that I have a small tent with me! Why don't we set it up here?" said Lily. "Great idea!" said Rose. They set up the tent; it looked so lovely. "I have three sleeping bags and one pillow with me. Can we put those in the tent, too?" asked Tina. "Of course, why not?" asked Rose.

After setting everything up, the cave looked as good as home. "Oh, I am so hungry. Let us eat something. This journey had tired me out," said Lily. "Yes, what do you want to eat?" asked Rose. "Cereal?" said Tina. "Cereal it is," replied Rose. "I am going to drink milk," said Lily. "How? We don't have milk!" said Tina. "I brought milk powder with me; we just need to mix it with water, and we will have milk," said Lily

The three girls ate breakfast and also gave Bella some milk as they didn't bring any food for her. "What is Bella going to do without her mom?" asked Tina. "I have no idea. I just hope everything works out," said Rose.

Back at home, Mom, Dad, Aunt, and Luna were safely rescued and are staying at a shelter. "I am so worried about the kids! Who knows what they are doing? How will they survive all alone? That too with a newborn kitten!" said Mom. "They did pack many things in their bags. Maybe they are safe somewhere," said Dad as he consoled Mom.

"Why don't we try calling their phones?" asked Aunt Bright. "Only Rose has a phone. Let me try calling it," said Dad as he called her phone. "It says no signal," said Dad. The rescue team desperately tried to find the kids, but it was all in vain.

Back at the island, the kids were having the best time of their lives setting up the cave. "Doesn't this rock look like a little table? The cave has a little crack above it. This is the perfect place to keep my solar-powered stove!" said Rose. "Yes, the crack will also work as a chimney!" said Lily.

"There are so many plants with berries. Why can't we pluck and eat them?" asked Tina. "Yes, we do need fresh fruit. We can't survive with only packed food," said Lily. "OK, I have my forest guide with me. Let's go eat the berries which are not poisonous," said Rose. "Who will look after Bella?" said Tina. "I am very tired, so I'll stay inside the cave with Bella. You two can go," said Lily.

"What does the guide say about wild berries?" asked Tina. "I'll just read out whatever it says," said Rose. "Blue, black, and purple skin is a good sign. Orange and red are 50/50. Avoid green, white, and yellow berries. Avoid bitter-smelling berries. Just because an animal eats a berry, don't eat it. It might be poisonous for you," read out Rose. "You know, I think we should go back to the cave. I don't think this is worth it," said Rose. "Yes, the ridiculously small number of calories in those berries are not worth getting poisoned. Let's go back," said Tina.

"What happened? Back so early?" asked Lily. "The guide said that the small number of calories in berries isn't worth it because if we accidentally eat a poisonous berry, we can get very sick," said Tina. "Yes, and we brought some food anyway," added Rose.

I hope you remember what day it is today," said Lily. "Your 13th birthday! Congratulations, Lily! You are now a teenager!" said Tina. "Too bad you have celebrated your birthday in a cave," said Rose. "No, I'm having the best time of my life! I feel like I'm in an adventure story!" exclaimed Lily.

"I'm quite hungry. Does anyone know what time it is?" asked Tina. "I don't know. My phone is not working. But I think it might be noon as it is scorching hot," said Rose. "Then come on, what are we waiting for? Let's make lunch!" said Lily. "Anything for the birthday girl!" said Rose. "The only food available for lunch is instant noodles," said Rose. "Well, then make it!" said Lily. "I want to help!" said Tina.

So, Rose turned on the stove, boiled some water made instant noodles for all of them, and gave some water to Bella. Everyone ate their lunch very quickly as they were hungry like a lion.

"I'm so grateful to have you as my elder sister, Rose," said Tina. "Why thank you!" said Rose. "So, you are not grateful to have me as your elder sister?" asked Lily jocularly. "What! No! I didn't mean it like that!" replied Tina. Rose and Lily laughed. "I think I'm getting homesick," said Rose. "What? You are getting sick of home?" asked Tina. "No, Tina, she means that she misses home very much," said Lily. "If that is the case, then I am homesick too," said Tina. "Well, who isn't?! It has been almost a whole day on this island," replied Lily. "Who knows for how long we will be stuck on this island?" said Tina. "I already told you! Don't lose hope! We have found ourselves a place to sleep, cook, and eat, so why are you worried?" asked Rose. "We can't live here forever!" said Tina. "We won't!" assured Lily

"Fine, but I'm bored now," said Tina. "Let's play chess! Oh, but it should have only two players... maybe snakes and ladders?" said Rose. "Sure," said Lily. "Yeah, why not?" said Tina. They all played games and slept to while away time.

Soon after everyone slept, a boy wearing a yellow shirt and blue shorts shouted at them. "Hey! What are you guys doing here? This is my island!" "Who are you?" said Tina. "My name is Cedar, and this is our private island. We have come here for vacation. With whose permission did you come here?!" said the boy angrily.

"I am sorry, Cedar. My name is Rose. We had an earthquake and a flood in our town. Due to the earthquake, our house broke into two, and we had to escape using a boat. But just as we got on the boat, the rope got cut, and we drifted till here. We crash-landed on this island this morning," explained Rose

"Do I look like I care?! I need you out of my island now!" shouted Cedar. "Then where are we supposed to go?!" shouted Lily. "Like I said before, I don't care! I am going to call my father here now," said Cedar as he ran to get his father. "What a silly name! His name is the name of a plant!" said Tina. "We have a lot more to worry about than his name, Tina!" said Rose.

"Don't be silly, Cedar! How can there be other people on this island? We have guards!" said Cedar's father. "No, Dad, I don't know where the guards went, but there are three girls who look about my age and also a kitten! Please listen to me!" said Cedar. The father went along with Cedar to find the girls. To his surprise, the guards were nowhere to be found, and there were indeed three girls and a kitten inside the cave.

"What on earth!? How did you all get in here? And where are my guards?!" asked Cedar's father. "They said that they crashed into our island this morning," replied Cedar. "Can you please let us know where we are now and how to get home?" asked Rose. "Sorry, but no, once you enter our island, you will never leave it," replied Cedar's father. "What will we eat? We will soon run out of provisions," said Lily. "We will provide you one meal a day," said Cedar's father as he left.

"Why, Dad, why can't we just kick them out?" asked Cedar. "Well, if we do that, they might tell everyone that we live here," replied Cedar's Dad. "So what?" asked Cedar. "You fool! We don't want anyone to know about our whereabouts," said Cedar's Dad. The girls had overheard this conversation and were very worried.

"Looks like we will never see our parents again!" said Tina. "No, we will escape somehow," assured Rose. "How on earth will we do that?!" said Lily. "Maybe spy on them?" said Tina. "Good idea! Then we will get to know what they are up to! Let's make a plan!" said Rose. "I'm scared. I will stay here with Bella and look after our stuff," said Lily. "Okay, scaredy cat," said Tina.

"Come on, Tina, let's follow them and find out where they live," said Rose. So, they started following them. While secretly following them, Tina accidentally stepped on a branch! "Shh! Can't you walk properly!" whispered Rose. "Who's that!" shouted Cedar's father. "Probably the wind or something," said Cedar. "What if it is one of the girls following us?!" said Cedar's father. Tina and Rose hid themselves behind a bush, hoping that Cedar and his father wouldn't find them. They looked everywhere but fortunately couldn't find the girls, so they left. "Phew!" whispered Rose. "Sorry, Rose, next time I will be more silent," said Tina.

The two girls followed Cedar and his father to the other side of the island to find a house and four guards guarding it. Once again, Tina made a noise by stepping on a dry leaf. "I am sure that someone is following us, Cedar!" shouted Cedar's father. "Who is there? Come out right now!" he shouted.

The two girls ran as fast as they could to the cave, but Tina tripped over a branch and twisted her ankle! "Ow!" cried Tina. "Don't worry, we will reach the cave," said

Rose. Tina was not able to move her leg, so Rose carried her to the cave. Both of them safely reached the cave, and after five minutes or so, Cedar and his father reached the cave.

"Were any one of you following us?!" he said angrily. All of them shook their heads to say no. "Those girls are behaving very suspiciously," said Cedar's father. "Oh, Dad, you are just paranoid! They are helpless, naïve girls! What can they do?" said Cedar. "You are right, Cedar; I'm worried for nothing!" said his Dad. So, Cedar and his father left the cave and continued to go to their house. "That was a close one!" said Rose. "How is your leg now, Tina?" asked Rose worriedly. "It is paining a lot!" said Tina. "It's all my fault. I should have made you stay here with Lily..." said Rose.

To soothe Tina's pain, Rose dipped her handkerchief in water and tied it to Tina's ankle. "Wow, this feels nice and cold," said Tina. "It's water. How would it not feel cold?" said Lily. "Try shaking your leg," said Lily. "I can't! It hurts!" replied Tina. "But I still can't believe that Rose carried me till here!" said Tina. "Me neither!" said Rose. "I think the sun is about to set," said Lily. "Let's eat something," said Tina. "What do you want to eat?" asked Rose. "Well, what is there to eat?" asked Tina. "The only food we have left are instant soup and cookies. "Might as well have the soup," said Tina.

Rose made instant soup for them by mixing the powder with hot water she made using the help of the stoves. All of them ate and slept. In the middle of the night, Rose woke up as she heard some noises. "Oh my god! What on earth is that noise?" she thought. "Maybe I should go and check it out!" She managed to climb the cave and sat on top of it. The moon was full and bright. She hid herself behind a palm tree's leaf.

She saw Cedar and his father talking with a guard. "Come on, Cedar, let us go and rob more houses." "Oh, this is going to be fun!" replied Cedar. "Look after our robbed goods well, I trust you. Don't even try to steal our gold. You know what happened to the other guard! We still have space in the dungeon," Cedar's father said to the man.

Then, both of them left on a ship. The ship had a big red light that woke Lily up. Lily, too, had the same idea of climbing up the cave to see what was happening. After she climbed up, she almost screamed as she saw Rose. "Shh! Don't make a noise! It's me, Rose." "Well, what are you doing here?" whispered Lily. "Let's climb down this cave, and then I'll tell you what I saw and heard," said Rose

They both climbed down the cave and went back inside. "You know what, I am very tired. You can tell me and Tina what happened tomorrow," said Lily. "Okay then, goodnight," said Rose. Tina was the one who got up the earliest. She shouted "Rose! Lily! Wake up! The sun is out!" said Tina.

"I am so worn out right now," said Rose. "I can't understand what you are trying to say," said Tina. "She is saying that she is tired," explained Lily. "Why? It's not like you stayed up all night! Did you?" asked Tina. "Well, yesterday night, some noise made me wake up," said Rose. "Ah yes, please tell us what happened," requested Lily.

"What do you mean?" asked Tina.

"As I said, some noise woke me up. I wanted to see what was happening, so I climbed up this cave and hid myself behind a leaf of a palm tree." "How on earth did you climb this cave?!" asked Tina. "I don't know. Maybe I can use my hands and legs," replied Rose jocularly. "Anyways, then I heard Cedar and his father talking to the guard," said Rose

"Oh wow! What did you hear?" asked Tina. "I found out that Cedar and his father are robbers! Also, I found out that there was another guard before this guard who tried to steal their robbed goods who got caught and now is in a dungeon." "Just as I was about to get down, Lily climbed up here," said Rose. "Yes, I saw a light come through that crack in this cave. So, I wanted to climb up there and find out what caused the light. I also noticed that Rose was missing. I climbed up to find Rose sitting there," said Lily

"Did you find out what was the light?" asked Tina. "Yes, we did. Cedar and his father left in a ship that had the big red light which I suppose was turned on accidentally," replied Rose. "We must do something about this," said Tina. "Yes, but what can we do?" asked Lily. "I'm starving! Let us eat something and then think this out," replied Rose.

"Poor Bella! I feel so bad for her! She had nothing to eat! She has only been drinking water for the past few days! She doesn't even have her mom with her," said Lily. "Yes, but there is nothing we can do!" replied Tina. "By the way, Tina, how is your leg?" asked Rose. "Oh, I forgot about it! It healed, I guess! Thank you so much for your help, sisters!" said Tina

"I want to escape this island somehow!" said Lily. "Well, I am so homesick. Why can't we just get in the boat with all our things and go wherever the tide takes us?" asked Tina. "Firstly, it is too dangerous. I would rather be homesick than seasick! And secondly, I want to do something about Cedar and his father!" replied Rose

"Rose, I think Tina's idea is better. And I don't think we can do anything about these robbers," said Lily. "Please, you do not want to do that! Here on this island, we found people and a house. We can ask someone for help too!" said Rose. "Oh, as if anyone will be able to help us!" said Tina. "But I suppose Rose is right too! But both your ideas are equally risky," responded Lily

Back in their hometown, the flood went away and their homes were fixed and cleaned. Mom, Dad, and aunt desperately tried to find their kids but it was of no use. It had been two whole days and since there was nothing heard from the girls, they lost all hope. They all thought that they would never see their little girls ever again. Even though Luna couldn't speak, you could see she missed her kitten deeply.

Bella looked so thin and weak as she did not eat any proper food and could not even see her mother. The girls felt so bad for her but what could they do? There was a shortage of food but the girls didn't want to have anything Cedar gave because who can trust robbers?

The day continued, and soon enough, the sun started to set. But the moon's light was so bright they could see their way. But this time, the girls decided to stay up all night to see what Cedar and his father would do.

They noticed that Cedar and his father left on a ship with red lights, just like yesterday. Rose came up with a plan. "Do any of you have sleeping pills? The ones that mom uses to go to sleep?" asked Rose. "Let me check," said Tina and Lily. "Well, you are in luck! I do have these for some reason. Why do you need these anyway? We planned to stay up the whole night!" said Lily

"It's not for me! It's for the guards!" said Rose. "What do you mean for the guards?" asked Tina. "Well, we are going to go there and sneak into the house!" said Rose. "How? They have guards!" asked Tina. "I have a plan! Please give me a cup of water!" exclaimed Rose. "Why does she need water?" the girl thought.

Rose powdered five of the sleeping pills and put them in the water. "Woah! That is too strong to take! Don't tell me you are planning to drink it!" said Lily. "No, silly! Just follow me, Tina. Please get in the cave and look after Bella and our stuff. Make sure that she doesn't run away!" ordered Rose. "But I want to come too!" said Tina. "I don't want you to get hurt like yesterday! No, be quiet and look after everything," said Rose.

"Lily, please follow me," Rose said. Rose was walking in the direction of Cedar's house. "Why are we going there?" asked Lily. "You'll see!" said Rose. Soon enough, she reached the house. "Hi, mister guard, you look tired," said Rose. "I suppose you are the girl the master was telling me about! I'm sorry, but you are strictly not allowed inside," replied the guard.

"Aww, too bad!" said Rose. "But you look so tired! Do you want to sip water?" "Oh, that is so sweet of you! I feel so bad that such a nice girl like you had to land on this island," said the foolish guard as he drank the water mixed with sleeping pills. The guard at once fell to the ground with a huge thump. "What a clever idea!" said Lily. "I told you! Come on! Let's sneak inside the house!" said Rose.

To her surprise, the house wasn't even locked! Both the girls went inside. "Rose, switch on the light!" said Lily. "I don't know where the switches are!" said Rose. The girls stumbled through the house until they found the switch. They switched on the lights. "Wow! These robbers are crazy rich!" said Lily as they explored the house. "Yes, so rich but doesn't have the common sense even to lock their house! No wonder the other guard stole their goods!" replied Rose with a laugh.

"Rose! Look! A telephone! Let us go check if it works!" said Lily. Both of them ran at the speed of light to the telephone. They eagerly dialed their mother's number. Back at home, Mother's phone rang loudly at night. "Who on earth will call at this hour?!" said Aunt Bright. "I don't know, but I want to pick it up," said Mom as she picked up the call.

"Hello? Mom?" the girls said eagerly. "Oh my gosh! "Is that you? Lily and Rose?" asked Mom. "Yes, we are! We are currently trapped on an island! Please help!" "How did you find a telephone on an island?!" "It's a long story! But can you just help us for now?" "Yes! I am going to tell the police bye." "Bye," said the girls.

Both of them were jumping with joy, but suddenly, they heard a faint cry for help. They followed the noise, and it led to a dungeon. It had a lock, and Rose somehow managed to open it with her hairpin. They found a man, about 20 years or so, inside the dungeon room. "Thank you so much for freeing me, dear kids! My master trapped me here two days ago! But who are you, and how did you get here?" he asked. Rose explained how they ended up on the island. The man was shocked. "Cedar's father robbed my house, and I caught him red-handed. But then I slept and woke up here. He told me to guard these robbed goods, but as I was trying to get back my goods, he caught me and put me inside this dungeon," he spoke.

Do you know where he keeps his goods?" asked Rose. "Look around!" said the man. Rose saw that that dungeon was full of gold. So, the girls called the police and told them everything. It was about five in the morning at that time.

Mom had already gone to the police station and given the number. The police somehow tracked the number and found out where the girls were. Before the sun rose, Cedar and his father returned to find their guard unconscious and the girls inside their house. He was furious.

"How dare you enter into my house and free the man that I imprisoned!" he shouted. Just as this was happening, the police entered the house with Tina and Bella. The police recognized Cedar's father and immediately arrested him. They also took the gold in their ship and told the girls to pack their things and get on the ship.

The girls packed up all their things and waved goodbye to Cedar's father. It was a long journey to get back home but it was so worth it! The three girls hugged their mother tight and Bella was finally reunited with her mom. Everyone's eyes were full of tears.

"Please tell us whatever happened these two-three days," requested Dad. The girls explained everything about how they crash-landed and then found out that they had landed on Cedar's Island, the robber, and so on. The police and the adults were shocked to hear this. "Dear children, thank you so much for reporting this criminal to us. You don't know how big of a criminal he is. He has robbed more than 500 houses!" said the police. "These girls are a brave pair," said the other policeman.

Soon, the girls were all over the news for being so brave and were now known as the brave trio. "This was such a fun adventure!" said Tina. "Yes, it was indeed!" replied Rose. "Especially since today is my birthday, this is the best birthday gift ever!" said Tina as she celebrated her birthday. "What is your wish, Tina?" asked Mom. "I wish for many more adventures like this!" said Tina.

Maybe they will have more adventures together! What do you think?

THE BRAVE TRIO (PART 2)

"Mom, I'm so bored! I have no idea what to do right now!" said Rose. "Remember what happened last year during summer?" asked Tina. "That's quite an adventure we will never forget, haha," said Lily. "This year, I want to learn crochet!" said Rose. "And I want to learn piano!" said Lily. "I want to learn how to solve Rubix cubes! I wonder what will happen this year?" asked Tina.

"Well... I kind of miss living on an island... remember the wild cats there! They were so cute!" said Rose. "Nah, dogs are better," said Tina. "Beep" "BEEP" "BEEP". "What is that noise?" asked Mom. "Oh wow! Look! We have new neighbors!" said Dad.

"Any kids there?" asked Lily. "Yes, I think I see a girl about your age," said Dad. "Dad, can we go and welcome them to this neighborhood?" asked Rose. "Yes, we should. That's such a sweet thing to do!" said Dad.

"Wait, I think I have an extra pie from yesterday, let's give them that as a gift!" said Mom. "That's nice, now come on let's go," said Dad. "Ding dong" they rang the doorbell. "Oh, good morning! We are your new neighbors, welcome to this town! We brought some homemade pie for you!" said Mom.

"Oh, that's so sweet! You didn't have to! Who are these cuties?" asked the new neighbor. "These are our daughters, Rose, Lily, and Tina," said Dad. "We have a little girl too. Let me go and get her," said the new neighbor.

"Oh, wow, she is super tall!" said Mom. "Yes! And what's with the suit?" asked Dad. "How would I know?" asked Mom. "Hello there, I'm Hisoki," said the new neighbor. "Nice to meet you, man! Are you Japanese?" asked Dad. "Yes, I am," said Hisoki.

"Hi! I'm Asteria! Do you girls want to play?" asked Asteria. "Sure!" said the girls in unison. "Come on in, we have a backyard you girls can play in," said Hisoki. "I didn't quite catch your name," said Mom. "Oh, sorry, my name is Lilith," said Lilith.

The girls went off to play. "How do you guys handle this extreme heat?!" asked Lilith. "I have a recipe for ice cream. Shall I teach you? It needs only three ingredients," said Mom. "Okay, come inside," said Lilith. "Umm, I'm about to watch the match. Do you want to join?" Hisoki asked. "Oh, you watch the match too. I would love to join!" said Dad.

"Asteria, your name sounds so beautiful! What is the meaning?" asked Rose. "Thank you! It means star," said

Asteria. "Why are your parents wearing suits?" asked Tina. "They are lawyers, so they wear suits," said Asteria.

"That's so cool!" said Lily. All of them played board games, etc, and enjoyed their time. The girls even talked about the adventure they had last year. "Rose, Lily, Tina! It's bedtime. We have to go!" said Mom. "Coming," said the girls.

"Goodnight," said Mom. "Goodnight, sweet dreams to all!" said Tina. All of them slept well. "Bang" "CRASH" "BANG". "Lily, do you hear that noise?" whispered Rose. "Probably the wind. Go to sleep, Rose," replied Lily.

The night was filled with random noises, which kept Rose awake. The next morning, they were awakened by the sound of their doorbell. "Who is at the door at this hour? It's just 6 AM," said Mom. "I'll go and check it out," said Dad. He opened the door to see Asteria crying and shivering.

"What happened to you? Are you all right? Come inside!" said Dad in a panic. She went inside their house. "Please help me! When I woke up, I saw our door open, windows broken, and my parents nowhere to be found!" said Asteria.

"Omg, I'll call the police! Meanwhile, come and have something to eat, calm yourself. I'm sure everything is fine," said Mom. Soon, the police arrived. "Little girl, did you find anything else odd in your house except the door and windows?" asked the police

"I found this letter, but it looks like a story, I have no idea what it means," said Asteria, handing them the letter. "Are you trying to prank us? Why would a criminal leave a children's story in a crime scene!" said the policeman.

"But it was there!" said Asteria. "We will try our best to find them," said the police. "Wait, isn't that the symbol of the biggest criminal gang in our city?" said a policeman. "Maybe they are trying to confuse us. Forget it. We need to find that girl's parents," said another policeman.

"Don't worry, Asteria. The police will find them soon," comforted Rose. But this letter! Maybe it's a clue!" said Asteria. Really? If you think so! Maybe we can find something out!" said Lily. "Mom, Dad, can Asteria, Rose, Lily, and I go to the local playground and play?" asked Tina.

"Okay, sure, come back in time for dinner," said Mom. The girls left for the park, which was not too far away. "Why are we here, Tina?" asked Asteria. "So that we can try and find out what the letter means!" said Tina. "Good idea! Asteria, can you read the letter for us?" asked Rose. "Yes," said Asteria.

"PLAY SCHOOL

LITTLE KIDS

SCHOOL TIME

HELICOPTER

ELEPHANT

LITTLE KIDS

PLAY SCHOOL."

Once upon a time, there lived a hare and a tortoise. The hare was always proud of its speed. One day, the hare challenged the tortoise to a race. It was so confident that it took the long way and told the tortoise to take the shortcut. The hare walked into the forest, a little far from the playground." "Wait," interrupted Lily. It says 'pls help'! The random words at the beginning of the letter!" said Lily

"And we have a forest a little bit far away from this playground, too! Girls, what are you waiting for? Let's go!" said Rose. "Read the next paragraph, Asteria," said Tina.

"The hare saw pine trees everywhere and realized it was lost. It went further in till the mango trees came in sight," said Asteria. "Let's go into the pine forest! Maybe there are mango trees after that!" said Rose. All of them went bravely into the pine forest. But they could not find mango trees anywhere.

"ROAR" "ROAR" they heard the sound. "Ahh! Is that what I think it is?!" asked Tina. "Yes! It's a lion! Girls, run!" screamed Lily. All of them ran aimlessly till they stopped hearing the roars of the lion. "I think we finally lost it!" said Rose. "Thank God! That was the scariest thing ever!" said Asteria.

"Girls! We are surrounded by mango trees! But where are we?" asked Tina. "Oh no, we're lost!" said Rose. "At this point, we might as well follow the letter! We have nowhere else to go!" said Lily. "OKAY, let me read the next paragraph," said Asteria.

"The hare saw a place, which was once filled with water but was now dry as a barn. It fell inside the place, not knowing what to do," said Asteria. "Was filled with water? Maybe it's a lake or pond!" said Lily. "But it's now dry as a barn... maybe it's like a dam or something," said Rose.

All of them went exploring the place when suddenly Tina disappeared. "Wait, where is Tina!" shouted Rose. "Omg, what have I done! We shouldn't have come here in the first place! We should have let the police do their job," said Rose. "Help! It's me, Tina," they heard a faint voice.

"Isn't that Tina's voice? It's coming from that direction! Come fast!" said Asteria. They all ran, to find a big hole. "Doesn't this look like an old well?" asked Rose. "Yes, that's what I was thinking about too!" said Lily. "So that means this is the place the hare fell into! Once filled with water, now dry as a barn!" said Rose.

"You're right, Rose! Look, Tina is down there! Hopefully, she isn't hurt!" said Asteria. The well wasn't that deep. But there was a rope. The girls used the rope to climb down the well. "Tina, are you okay?" asked Rose. "Yes, but I think I hurt my left hand a little. It hurts," said Tina

"Well, we are in the middle of nowhere. Do you think you can manage it?" asked Lily. "Yes, I think so," said Tina. "OKAY, so the next part of the letter says:

The hare knocked on the walls to find a pathway. Inside was the end of the race. The hare found the tortoise sitting there already. It now knows that slow and steady wins the race," said Asteria. "And that's the end of the letter too," she said.

"Then let's knock the walls too!" said Lily. The girls started knocking on the walls of the well. Suddenly, Rose found a wall that sounded hollow when knocked. "Girls, I think this is a fake wall! Can we all try to kick it together?" said Rose.

"Yes, sure," said Asteria. And sure enough, they found a pathway that led to a locked door. "Maybe we can open the lock with my hairpin!" said Tina. "As if that would work!" said Lily. But Tina somehow managed to open the lock. "Rose, I'm scared," said Asteria.

"Okay, I'll go in first," said Rose. They went inside the door to find Asteria's mom and dad. "Mom! Dad! Are you okay?" said Asteria. "We are fine, kids. Can you please untie us from this chair," said Hisoki. They untied them when suddenly two men armed with guns barged inside.

"Kids, you will pay for this!" said a man. "How many of you are there? Three? Haha, three weak girls! What an easy target!" said the man. Suddenly, Rose, who was hiding behind the door at that time, attacked the men from the back and snatched their guns. "No, you will pay for this!" said the girls.

Rose shoots the man in the leg. Though they were alive, they couldn't move. The men desperately called their leader. "Sir! Some four girls came out of nowhere, took our guns, and shot us!" said the man.

"What! How can you be defeated by kids? Are you stupid?! I'm 10 hours away from the city! Do something, you idiots! Don't let them escape!" said the leader. "Oh my, we are screwed! My leg is bleeding! I can't even walk!" said the man

"Come on! Let's lock the door and get out of here!" said Lilith. They all locked the door and climbed up the rope. "Thankfully, I have my phone with me! The kidnappers didn't know that though!" said Hisoki. They called the police. They managed to track their location and rescue them.

"Girls, thank you so much. They are one of the biggest criminal gangs in this city," said the policeman. "We have to tell this to Mom and Dad!" said Rose. "Don't worry, we are heading towards the town court. We have arrested these criminals," said the police

"Dear girls! We were worried about you! It's 6 PM, we searched the playground, and you were not there! We called the police, and they informed us that you were stuck in a forest! You didn't even inform us!" said Dad. "Sorry, Mom and Dad... we knew that you wouldn't allow us to go to a forest, so we kind of lied to you," said Lily. "This won't happen again, I promise!" said Rose.

The criminals kidnapped the lawyers as they were secretly planning a lawsuit against them. The mother overheard the conversation of the criminals and wrote a secret letter with the criminal's symbol in a way that the criminals weren't smart enough to notice. The kids won an award from the Mayor for their bravery and courage. They honored the three girls as even last year; they caught one of the most wanted criminals. These girls were all over the news and were known as the brave trio.

BORN HEROS

BORNHEROES

"Haiya!" shouted Lexi. "Lexi, you are the best girl in this class. But you have to be firmer, sound, and look confident," said her karate master. "Yes, master," she replied. "Lexi, you are going to a national-level competition. I think you need more training. Is it OKAY if you stay here and practice till 8 PM?" said the master. "But master, I have been practicing since 4! I'm quite tired," said Lexi. "To succeed, you have to work hard," said her master. Lexi practiced for hours. Then, finally, it was time to go home. She rushed home in her cycle as she had homework waiting for her at home.

"I'm home, Leo! Oh, come on! He's gone out again? Why does this always happen to me?!" said Lexi as she removed her shoes. "Why is he never home!" She called her brother. "The person you are trying to reach is currently unavailable. Please try again later." "Ugh! I'm all alone again! What should I do? I'm gonna take a nap," said Lexi as she drowsed off.

[at midnight] "Lexi? LEXI!" shouted Leo, only to find her sleeping on the couch. "LEO! Where on earth do you go?! You always leave me alone! I fell asleep soon after I finished my karate class at 8 PM! I tried calling you, but it said it was unavailable!" said a frustrated Lexi.

"I'm sorry, Lexi, I had to do some urgent work, by the way... I kept your dinner in the fridge. Did you eat it?" said Leo. "No, why is your hand covered in scratches?" "Umm, no reason? Maybe I got them while making you dinner!" said Leo as he hurriedly covered his hand with a jacket. "Weird... I didn't know someone could hurt themselves while making pasta..." said Lexi as she ate her dinner at midnight.

"Can you help me with my math homework? Trigonometry is confusing!" asked Lexi. "I'm tired.... But okay, will do," replied Leo. Leo was the math genius. Even if someone woke him up from his sleep and asked a math question, he would be able to answer it immediately. "So, you divide the sin by cos, and there you go! That's your answer!" explained Leo

"You know, Leo... sometimes you're the best brother I could ask for. But I just don't understand where you disappear suddenly... most of the time during the night," said Lexi. "Aw, thanks, Lexi, you're the best sister too," said Leo as he tucked her in bed

Leo and Lexi lived together in a small apartment. Lexi had no idea about who her parents were, why they were not here etc. Sometimes she got curious and asked her brother, but he used to ignore her questions saying, "As long as we are together, you have nothing to worry about."

Lexi performed well in school. She always had the highest grade in class, was good in sports and arts, and had what's called the 'perfect life', but she used to feel lonely and distant from her family. Lexi was very strong. She has won multiple championships in karate. One day, "Tomorrow is Mother's Day! All your mothers are invited to the party tomorrow!" said her teacher. Her brother came with her for Mother's Day. She saw all the kids with their parents, and she asked, "Leo, do I have a mother or father?"

"Yes, you do. You have both!" replied Leo. "Why aren't they here? Do they not like me?" "No, it's not like that... it's just that they are very busy with work." "Too busy for me?" "Umm, wow, look! Cake! Let's go have some!" replied Leo. Leo tried to avoid these conversations by redirecting her to something else.

"Good morning, Lexi!" said Leo. "GM Leo," replied Lexi. "What's GM?" "It stands for the good morning; how do you not know that?" "Idk. Do you know what day it is?" asked Leo. "It's Sunday? That's why I need not go to school today!" replied Lexi

"No, what's the date today?" asked Leo. "The 24th." "And that is?" "Oh! It's my birthday! Gosh, I'm an idiot! It took me so long!" said Lexi with a laugh. "You sure are. Haha. I planned a whole day of fun just for you. First, we're going to go to the trampoline park!" said Leo.

"Yay!" said Lexi. Lexi was a strong girl. By strong I mean very strong, she could lift twice her weight, do backflips, and excel at sports. No one knew why. Her brother wasn't a sporty guy either, everyone thought that she was a miracle. She would excel at a sport even if it was her first time.

"Breaking news: a gang of eight tried to kidnap a little girl at approximately 9 PM-12 AM. An unidentified person rescued her while defeating the criminals. Eight of them were found injured and unconscious, but the girl was found in a safe condition."

"Wow, there are so many criminals in this area! Right, Leo?" asked Lexi. "Umm, yeah. Look, there is a kitten outside! Isn't it so cute?" asked Leo. "Yes, it is…" said Lexi. "Hmm, why is my brother behaving so mysteriously suddenly? Is he a part of a gang? Is he a criminal? Or maybe… Maybe my suspicions are wrong. I guess I should try to enjoy my birthday in peace," she thought to herself.

The next morning, she went to school. "Good morning, kids. Be nice to your new classmate… Alexa!" said the teacher. "Hi everyone! Nice to meet you all!" said Alexa. "You can sit next to our class topper, Lexi. Lexi, show her around the school, okay?" said the teacher. "Okay, miss, I will," assured Lexi.

"Hey, Lexi, right?" "Yup, Alexa, you want me to show you around the school now?" "Nah, I want to get to know you… So, how's your family and life at home?" "It's complicated… I live with my brother in a small apartment… I don't know who my parents are… but it's cool." "That sounds fishy. Are you sure that your 'brother' is your real brother?" asked Alexa.

"Yeah, I guess. What else could he be?" replied Lexi. "You know, maybe a kidnapper? Just like what happened to Rapunzel?" "That's just a cartoon. Besides, he's the best brother ever." "If you think so, does he do anything suspicious?" "Well, sometimes he disappears at night and comes back in the morning," said Lexi. "I wouldn't trust him if I were you," said Alexa.

Lexi started to get curious. Back at home...ding! Leo heard a text message. "Tonight's a tough one, be ready – Dad." "Can I call you?" texted back Leo. Ring ring, ring ring, his phone rang. "Hi, son, what's the matter?" "Dad, Lexi is getting curious. She is 14. I don't think I can hide things from her anymore," said Leo

"She's just a naïve little girl. It can't be that bad." "But I want her to know the truth..." "You managed to hide things from her for more than a decade; I think you can handle this well." "She is going to find out somehow? Right?" asked Leo. "Until then, let her live her life at peace." "But, Dad, I started working with you at 14... why can't she too?" asked Leo

"She is a girl; she needs to be protected. We don't want her to get into trouble, and we don't want her to get us into trouble by telling her friends," replied Dad. "Btw what time should I come today?" "Come at 8 PM sharp." "That's hard..." "You have no choice." "That's true..." replied Leo while ending the call.

Soon, the day ended, and the school bell everyone was waiting for finally rang. "Hi brother, surprised you're early for once!" said Lexi. "Yeah, I didn't have work stuff today," replied Leo. "Hmm, what's the so-called 'work' you do?" asked Lexi. "You know, running here and there like that," replied Leo.

"Why do you work at night?" asked Lexi. "It's nothing. I just work night shifts a lot... leave that. Look, I just got a new tattoo! It's a tiger and a lion with fiery eyes, doesn't that look cool?" said Leo. "Cool, who are the tiger and the lion?" asked Lexi. "Well, the tiger is you, and the lion is me," replied Leo.

"That's cute... I'm starving, it's 6 PM already?! I have to get started on my essay! Hmm... what's for dinner?" asked Lexi. "What do you want?" Leo asked back. "What about... cheese toast and vanilla cupcakes for dessert?" said Lexi. "Wow, that's specific and unhealthy! But sure. Since you don't eat this often, I'll make it happen today," assured Leo.

"Oh brother, I don't know what to think about you. You're so mysterious and reserved, and it seems like you hide a lot of things from me. But on the other hand, you're always so sweet. You always get me what I want, no matter how hard it is to get. You're just so confusing to understand, even if I try so hard..." Lexi thought.

"Here's your dinner, princess!" said Leo. "Thanks!" replied Lexi. "Oh no! Is that the time? I have to go! Sorry and bye!" said Leo in a hurry. Lexi was used to this by now. She went on about her day and soon went to sleep. [At 4 AM] "creak" "boing" "creak" "What on earth is that noise? It must be my brother. Let me just pretend to sleep," Lexi thought to herself.

Lexi saw her brother covered in bruises. She was really worried. She didn't even know what to think. Her brother was giving first aid to himself. As soon as she went to bed again, she heard some noises. She peeped through the keyhole and saw her brother talking with a man. "It was tough…" "You did great today, don't worry, you're going to be fine. You have strength in your blood, just like me. Now I better get going before Lexi sees me," said the man.

"What the… who is that? And how does he know my name? I'm so scared; I have to do something, or else I will be scared like this forever," Lexi thought.

The next morning at 7 AM, she found her brother sleeping, looking exhausted. "Leo? Leo! Wake up!" said Lexi. "I'm really tired, Lexi. I'm not feeling well today. There are fruit loops and milk in the fridge," replied Leo with a tired voice. "What about lunch?" asked Lexi. "I have kept some money for lunch in your purse."

"What about school?" asked Lexi. "Can you ask if any one of your friends is willing to pick you up? I'm sorry, Lexi. This has never happened before, and it won't happen again. Please let me just take some rest, just for today… I need to go back to work again tonight," said Leo.

She ate her breakfast and went to school on her own. She was confused, scared, and didn't know what to do. Soon enough, school ended. Time flew by, and she walked home by herself. She went to karate class, came back, and started to paint some pictures to distract herself.

At about 9 PM, again, she saw her brother leaving. "Bye, Lexi, off to work," said Leo. "No problem, I'm so tired, I just want to sleep! Goodnight!" replied Lexi.

She put on one of her brothers' black jackets and wore a black mask. She wore some sneakers and went outside the house. There, she found her brother putting on a black hoodie and a mask. She slowly went behind her brother. "What place is he going to? A bank? At night? Is he going to rob the bank?" Lexi thought to herself.

"I know! How crazy! Someone with a lion-tiger tattoo just jumped in and saved my life!" she heard a voice from one of the coffee shops. She knew her brother had a tattoo like that but didn't think much of it. She then stepped on a dry leaf. Her brother turned sharply. He knew something was off.

"Thank goodness! Leo didn't see me! Or I don't know what he would do to me!" Lexi thought. Soon, they reached the bank. She saw a group of 20 people; some were stealing from the bank, and the others were stealing from innocent people on the street. Frightened, she hid behind a tree. She saw the same man she saw last night. He and her brother were fighting with the robbers. She couldn't believe her eyes. Her brother was very powerful. He could defeat so many people easily. Some of the robbers left the money and ran for their lives. She thought that her hiding spot was good. But soon, she was hit in the head.

"Ahh! Help! Leo! help!" Lexi shouted. "What?! Lexi?! Don't worry, I'm coming for you!" said Leo as he ran after her. Leo and his Dad saw her and a man fighting. Lexi managed to pin the man to the ground, but then the leader of the robbers tried to kidnap her... he tried to make her smell some powder, but she threw it on his face instead. "Little girl, you'll pay for this!" said a voice from behind. Lexi fought bravely and somehow managed to win the fight! But due to her injury, she fell unconscious. "She's a strong girl indeed," said Dad. "She sure is. Let's take her to the hospital," said Leo.

We need not worry about the two men, as they fled as soon as they saw Leo and his Dad, Cougar. A few hours later, Lexi woke up and was ready to go. She saw Leo and Cougar looking worriedly at her. All three of them were speechless. All were shocked about what just happened. Cougar drove the car, to a place where Lexi had never been to.

"Ariel, me and Leo are home... along with Lexi," said Cougar. "What? Why? How?" "I'll explain now... Leo, go to your room and take Lexi with you," said Cougar in an angry tone. "Your room? Leo, who are these people? Are these our parents?" asked Lexi. Leo was quite angry. "What made you think that following me was a good idea?! Were you out of your mind?!" shouted Leo.

"But—" "But what?! Look at you! Covered in injuries! Why would you even think about following me at night? This is nothing. There could have been so many things that might have happened! I thought you were a smart girl!" shouted Leo.

Lexi was rethinking her actions. She had never seen her brother get this angry before. Leo, on the other hand, was very tense. Soon, Ariel and Cougar came into the room. Cougar shouted at Leo, "Leo, you managed to take care of her for 14 years. Could you not see that someone was following you?! Don't you know to lock your doors?!"

Seeing all this, tears started streaming down Lexi's face. She was crying because she was just so confused. Leo hugged her. "I'm sorry I yelled at you, Lexi, but you must know that you should not have done what you did," said Leo. Ariel said, "Lexi dear, we're your real parents. I'm Ariel, your mother, and he is Cougar, your father."

"We are a family who save other people. We keep the world safe by putting our lives at risk," said Cougar. "But why did you leave me? Why am I living with my brother? Why can't I join you all too?" asked Lexi. "You are a girl. I just wanted to protect you from the world. We didn't want you to know about this because we knew you would want to join. But after seeing your skills, I'm quite amazed," answered Cougar.

"I am interested in becoming one of you all. I want to fight and put the bad people in their place," said Lexi.

"Leo! You lied to me for my whole life! I trusted you! I knew you were up to something, but why did you all have to lie to me? Do you have any idea how curious I was or how scared I was?! I saw what happened last night, you, covered in bruises, talking to 'Dad', etc. I even had the thought that I was adopted or maybe kidnapped?!" shouted Lexi.

"Lexi, it was my fault. I instructed your brother to raise you in a normal environment. I didn't have common sense back then. I thought that girls were good for nothing. But now, I have opened my eyes. Please, accept us as your parents," said Cougar.

"It's fine. I see your point of view. Most people are like that. I forgive you both," said Lexi. "You're one amazing little girl! Proud of you!" said Ariel. "I'm not little, I'm 14!" said Lexi.

"Lexi, I know it's a lot to take in... the reason I disappeared at night is that I was rescuing people in need. It's a hard job... that's why I was exhausted yesterday. But I just want you to know that I love you so much, and I want nothing but to give you a wonderful life. Please don't think of me as a liar, even though I was one," said Leo.

"It's okay, Leo. You were always the best brother I could ever ask for. It is pretty shocking to me that you managed to hide this from me my whole life. But I know that you're my brother. My only and best brother," said Lexi.

Soon, they all lived together in their own house. Lexi was happy to know that she had parents and wasn't kidnapped or something like that. "Lexi, I'm more than impressed by your skills. Do you want to join us? We can save people and be heroes!" asked Cougar.

"Yes, I told you that I was interested the second I met you all!" said Lexi. "Lexi, it's risky. And the training for it is quite hard. Are you sure you want to do this?" asked Leo. "You chose to do it, right?" asked Lexi. "Well, I didn't get much of a choice... but yes, it sure feels good to send the bad people to their place," said Leo.

"I don't mind that," said Lexi. "Lexi dear, I have to warn you. It's not as easy as it looks, and we are doing this anonymously," said Ariel. "It's okay. I know that it's the right thing to do, and I'm afraid of no one," said Lexi.

"Proud to see the sister I raised so brave!" said Leo.

Not too long after, Lexi underwent training for a few years and started to work with her family at night. Sometimes, she regretted her decision and wished to go back when she was thirteen. But this is her life now. She is one of the strongest people in her class, she still manages to get first rank. "Wow, I come from a family of lions and tigers... in human form!" she thought.

"But I just have one question: Why don't you just join the police? You can help the world that way," said Lexi. "Well, we don't want to have problems with the general public, and we don't want to be included in politics?" said Ariel. "Why do you do this anonymously?" asked Lexi. "Well, it's just easier to do. We don't want to be interviewed and become famous! It's quite the drama!" said Cougar. "That makes sense, but it's kind of odd... if we showed ourselves who we are, maybe we can inspire people and maybe even open a martial arts training center," said Lexi. "We haven't thought of that yet; besides, we are too old to run a business!" said Ariel. "Maybe I can do that...," said Lexi. Soon, Lexi won the national championship and was known everywhere for her strength. The Mayor offered her the position of police to honor her.

Years pass by. You might wonder where Lexi is now and what she is doing with her life. Lexi is now one of the most popular policewomen, known for her strength and bravery. She opened a martial arts training center, which is always fully booked. She fought and gave all the criminals a lesson they would never forget. She and her family live in a big mansion. They are always all over the news with the title 'born heroes'.

[MORAL: Lexi's parents thought that Lexi was just a girl and was not capable of anything. But she was way stronger than anyone expected her to be. Strength has no age or gender.]

THE EPIC ADVENTURES OF CANDACE AND VALARIE

CHAPTER 1

❤

TILL MIDNIGHT TO RETREAT

"Kids, I hope you enjoyed this school year. It's too bad that it has come to an end now! Hope to see you all in 10th grade. Enjoy your summer vacation!" said the teacher. "Thank you, mam! Happy holidays to all! I hope all of you will have a great vacation!" said Valerie. "Yes, I will miss all of you so much! Bye!" shouted Lily, a classmate of the twins. The bell rang, and all the kids excitedly packed their things and got ready to go home.

There were two best friends, Candace and Valarie. They were so close that everybody called them the twins. They were cousins but looked so alike. Valarie's parents were out of town, so she had to live with Candace for a few days.

"It's both sad and happy that we are going to high school next year!" said Candace. "Yes, all the memories we made in middle school are now over. But you know, days fly! Let's just hope that next year will be a good one!" said Valerie. "Yeah, Hey, look! My mom has come to pick us up!

Let's go!" replied Candace.

"Hi, Mom!" the teens said together. "Hello! How was your last day at school?" said Mom. "It was fun," replied Candace. "Why the long face?" asked Mom. "Nothing, it's just that I enjoyed 9th grade so much that I don't want to leave it," replied Candace. "Well, time goes by! Don't worry, 10th grade will be an amazing year!" replied Mom.

"Mom, I think you're driving in the wrong direction," said Valerie. "Oh yeah, I forgot to tell you! We are going to visit your grandma!" said Mom. "We have a grandma?" asked the kids together. "How come we didn't know about that?!" said Valerie in shock. "She has always lived abroad, but now, since she came to our country, we are going to visit her. I think I have never told you about her! My bad!" replied Mom

"So, this grandma is your mom?" asked Candace. "Yes, Candace," replied Mom. "I'm so excited to meet her!" said Valerie. "Me too!" said Candace. "Okay, here we are! But we have to walk till there. Because our car won't fit here," said Mom. "OKAY, but Where are we? Grandma's house is so close to ours!" said Valerie. "Yes, it is indeed close to our house! This is 5th Cross Street; her house number is 24. This is just two streets away from our house!" said Mom. While walking, Candace found a weird rock. It was shaped like a perfect square. Candace curiously picked it up and showed it to Valerie. "Wow, what a cool rock! Let's keep it!" said Valerie. "Of course, I will keep it for now," replied Candace.

They went inside the huge house; it didn't even have a doorbell. They knocked on the door, and Grandma answered. "I was just about to visit your house! Wow! Look at you both! Grown so tall!" said Grandma. "You know us?" said Candace. "Yes, of course, dear! Come inside, everyone!" said Grandma. "Something is off about this grandma; I can feel it," Candace whispered to Valerie. "Yes, how come Mom has never told us about her? This place looks scary!" replied Valerie.

They talked for a while and soon got ready to leave. "I don't like Grandma at all. It's like she is some sort of evil being!" said Candace. "Yes, and that house looked so haunted! I hope we never go back there again!" said Valerie. "Hey, look! This rock has a hole! And it looks like a keyhole!" said Candace. "Oh yes! It does look like a keyhole!" replied Valerie. "Okay, girls, time to leave!" shouted Mom. "Coming!" shouted the girls.

While they were walking back to the car, Candace found another rock in the same place she found that square rock. But this time, it was shaped like a key! "Valerie! Look at what I found!" exclaimed Candace. "What? Another cool rock?" asked Valerie. "Yes, but this time it's a key!" replied Candace. "Wait, what! Let me see! Wow! It does look like a key! Maybe it fits that keyhole!" said Valerie. "We'll find that out later. Anyways, time to get in the car!" said Candace

"Mom, I'm hungry. Can we buy snacks on the way home?" asked Candace. "No, I already bought some snacks for you," replied Mom. "Okay then," said Candace. They reached home, had snacks, and even dinner! Then, it was time to sleep. "Mom, can you tell me a story?" asked Candace. "What?! We are too old for bedtime stories!" said

Valerie. "No, you're not! Both of you will always be my babies!" said Mom. "So, is that a yes?" asked Candace. "Haha, okay, I'll tell you a story!" said Mom.

"So once upon a time there lived a monster, it was called 'the monster of places'. It is known to put people in cages with bombs! Mostly in a parallel universe! It is known for correcting people, for example, you should never go into a stranger's house. Even if nothing happens, this monster will get you and trap you until you realize your mistake. But this is just a legend. When I was small, I used to be so scared of this silly monster," said Mom. "What kind of a story is that?" asked Candace. "Well, it's the only thing I can think of. Now off to sleep!" said Mom. "Okay, goodnight, Mom!" said the girls. "Good night," said Mom

The night flew by. Soon, it was morning. The girls woke up, got ready for the day, and sat down for breakfast. "So, what are we doing today?" asked Valerie. "Well, me and your father are going out for the day! So, you're going to be home alone. Is that okay?" asked Mom. "Yeah, sure! We will be fine! Won't we, Candace?" "Yes, of course! Enjoy your day!" said Candace.

"OKAY, we are leaving now! Bye!" said Mom. "Now? Okay then, bye!" said Candace. "Bye, Mom and Dad!" said Valerie. "Hey, why don't we take a look at those cool rocks you found yesterday?" said Valerie. "Sure, why not?" said Candace. "I hope it fits!" "Me too!" "It fits! It fits!" exclaimed Candace. "Open it!" shouted Valerie. "It has... a set of instructions?" "What do you mean, Candace?" "Look!" "Oh, it does!" said Valerie.

"It says that underneath this paper is a teleportation device! How cool!" said Candace. "Show me!" said Valerie. It was a rock that was shaped like a horn. "Well, how do we use it?" asked Valerie. "It says to hold this rock tightly in your right hand, close your eyes, then say the names of the people you want to teleport with, and then the name of the place we want to go to!" "Can I try it?" asked Valerie. "Sure, but I will choose the place," said Candace. "Okay, no problem," said Valerie.

"Where do you want to go?" "The park!" "Okay then." "Valerie, Candace. Park," said Valerie. "Ow!" the girls shouted. "Are you all right?" asked a boy. "Ah! Who are you? Where are we?" asked Candace. "I'm Tom. You are at the park, but how did you get here? Through thin air?!" said the boy. "Long story short, we teleported here," said Candace. "Oo, tell me all about it!" said Tom. The girls explained what happened. They also told him about their weird grandma.

"Wow! Well, that was interesting!" said the boy. "You both look tired! Why don't I buy you some ice cream?" said Tom. "Well..." said Valerie. "Come on! Is being kind illegal? I won't take no for an answer! Come on, let's go!" said Tom. "Okay, fine," agreed Valerie, thinking that Tom was just a sweet kid, but little did she know...

As soon as the girls ate the ice cream given by Tom, they felt dizzy and fell to the ground with a huge thud. When they woke up, both of them were locked in a cage. Below the cage, there were ferocious dogs with sharp teeth! The first one to wake up was Candace. "Ahh! Who are you? Where am I?! Wait, what?! Tom?!" screamed

Candace. "Yes, it's me. What were you silly girls thinking? Who would accept food from a stranger?!" said Tom. Tom clapped. He turned into a monster with one horn! Valerie woke up due to the noise. "I knew I shouldn't have trusted you! I'm such a fool!" said Valerie in despair.

"Who do we have here? If it isn't the twins!" "Grandma?!" shouted the girls in shock. "I knew it! I knew that something was off about you!" shouted Candace. "You can't do anything now! Silly girl! You're trapped! That bomb will explode at midnight, and both of you will be gone! Hahaha!" said the evil woman. "Unless we escape!" whispered Valerie. "Oh no, you won't; there's fire underneath you; either way, you won't survive! Buh-bye!" said the monster.

"Come on! Do something! You're the one who found that stupid rock!" said Valerie. "We're doomed! There's nothing we can do now!" said Candace. "No, we can at least try! Give me your hairpin! I'll try to open this lock!" said Valerie. "And then what? Fall in the fire?" asked Candace. "I'll figure that out later! Give me!" shouted Valerie. "Here you go," said Candace as she handed over the pin to Valerie.

"Yes! I opened it!!" shouted Valerie after she opened the lock. "Now what?" asked Candace. "Let's try to jump over the fire!" said Valerie. "No way! That's too far!" said Candace. "It's worth a try!" said Valerie. "Fine!" replied Candace. They tried to jump, but they missed. "Ahh! We're falling in the fire!" shouted Candace. "No!" shouted Valerie. Both of them screamed as hard as they could. All of their hard work went in vain.

"Girls, are you all right?!" asked Dad. "Wait, what?!" said Valerie. "Both of you were sleeping, and suddenly you started screaming. Are you all right?" asked Mom worriedly. "We're safe!" exclaimed Candace and hugged Valerie. "what's going on?" asked Mom. "Mom, we went to Grandma's house yesterday, right? We found two rocks, a lock, and a key," said Candace.

"Candace, your grandma lives on the other side of the world!" said Mom. "What do you mean?" asked Valerie. "Yesterday, 5th Cross Street, house number 24?" said Valerie. "Valerie, my mom lives with my sister far, far away. I'm sure I'll know if she comes here," said Mom. "Wait, let me google that address," said Dad. "It shows that it is an abandoned house," said Dad. "I'm so confused right now!" said Candace. "Same here!" said Valerie. "Yesterday, after school, we went straight to home," said Mom

"Yes, then both of you ate snacks, dinner, and slept!" said Dad. "What about the monster of places?" asked Candace. "Yes, I did tell you about that. Oh, maybe it was all just a dream!" replied Mom. "But if it was a dream, how did they know that address? They have never been there?" asked Dad. "Maybe it was a coincidence. Now I'm getting tired. Goodnight, you both!" said Mom. "I think I'll sleep with the light on," said Candace. "Okay," replied Mom.

After Mom left, Valerie felt uncomfortable. So, she checked under the pillow to find that square-shaped rock and a note but no key. The note read, "Hope you learned your lesson!"

Maybe it was a dream – or was it?

[MORAL: They got into this mess by accepting food from a random boy. You should never accept food from strangers, no matter their age]

CHAPTER 2

ROOM NO. 000

"Oh, I'm so tensed right now!" said Valarie. "Why? We studied everything!" said Candace. "But still!" said Valarie. "I have an idea. Why don't we go for a late-night drive?" suggested Candace. "Are you crazy? Our final is tomorrow!" said Valarie. "We can go and relax ourselves?" "Well, my parents will not let me, so don't even think about it. Besides, are you even old enough to drive?" asked Valarie. "I'm 15, and I have a permit," answered Candace. "Why don't you tell your parents that you're having a sleepover?" said Candace. "It's not the best idea," replied Valarie. "Oh, come on! You only live once!" said Candace. "Hmm, I don't think it's a good idea... fine, why not?" said Valarie.

Then, Valarie told her parents that she was having a sleepover at her friend's house to study and went to have a late-night car ride. "[music blasting] See! I told you it is a good idea!" exclaimed Candace. "I'm having fun, but I don't have a good feeling about this..." replied Valarie. "What is wrong with you? Come on, cheer up!"

said Candace. "Fine, only if you play my favorite song!" said Valarie. The girls were having so much fun together that they didn't even notice the time fly.

"OMG, Valarie!" shouted Candace. "What happened?" replied Valarie. "Look at the time!" "Oh my! This is bad! We should return home immediately!" said Valarie. "It's past midnight, and I'm so tired! I don't want to drive more," said Candace. "What are you going to tell your parents!" exclaimed Valarie. "They're out of town. And late-night driving is a risk. I don't want to get into an accident!" said Candace. "Well, this is all your fault! Now, what are we going to do? Sleep in the car?" said Valarie.

"No, let's go to a hotel and get a room for the night," said Candace. "I knew I should not have agreed to this! But fine, let's go to a hotel to sleep there for the night," said Valarie. Hours passed by, and they were driving on an unknown road and didn't find any hotels nearby. "Oh! What kind of place is this?! There are no hotels nearby!" said Candace. "Wait, I think I see one," said Valarie. "Where?" asked Candace. "That yellow light, I can see a big building!" said Valarie. "Oh wow! A 5-story hotel? For sure, they must have rooms available for us!" said Candace. "Well, then, what are you waiting for? Let's go," said Valarie

"This place looks so weird!" said Valarie. "I agree! We must walk on this very narrow street to get to the hotel! Our car won't fit here," said Candace. "I hope the car stays safe here," said Valarie. "Is your phone working?" asked Candace. "No, it shows no signal. Why?" asked Valarie. "Well, mine too; I don't know this place. I was hoping to see Google Maps to see where we are," replied Candace. "So, you're telling me that we are lost?" said Valarie. "I'm afraid so..." replied Candace.

"I'm so scared! This hotel looks old!" said Candace. "It's your fault we're stuck here anyway. Now move," said Valarie as she entered the hotel. "Hi sir, do you have any rooms available tonight?" asked Valarie. "Hello, my name is Rob, and I'm the receptionist working here; we have only one room available," said Rob. "Would you kindly provide the details of the room?" requested Valarie. "Sure, it's a double bedroom with a view of the whole city," said Rob. "That is wonderful, we'll take it. How much does that cost?" asked Valarie

"Oh no, in our hotel, it's a policy that only after we provide you service do we accept money. So, you can pay us tomorrow morning when you leave the hotel," said Rob. "How did you know that we're leaving tomorrow?" asked Candace. "Oh, it was just a guess," replied Rob. "Could you show us the way to our room?" asked Valarie. "Sure, just take the lift to the 5th floor. Your room number is 000," said Rob. "What a weird room number," said Candace. "Yeah, I thought they number their rooms starting from the ground floor. Maybe they number it from the last floor?" said Valarie

"What a small lift!" exclaimed Valarie. "Yes! It definitely can't fit more than two people! How does such a big hotel manage everything with this lift?! It's rusted too!" said Candace. "I know, right? I feel so uncomfortable here," said Valarie. "Yes, same here, but there's nothing we can do. We were lucky enough to find a hotel with available rooms at 2 AM!" said Candace. "I suppose you're right," replied Valarie

The lift took quite a while to get to the 5th floor, but the girls didn't bother about it. Eventually, they reached the fifth floor. "Finally! I can't wait to lay in that bed!" said Candace. "Well, we need to find our room first! It's such a big floor!" said Valarie. "Oh my, it certainly is!" agreed Candace. It took a while to find their room. It's because the 5th floor had 50 rooms in total. "50 rooms on one floor? They are rich, all right!" said Candace. "For sure!" said Valarie.

"This hotel be doing business all right! If there are 50 rooms on just one floor, imagine how many rooms five floors would have!" exclaimed Candace. "I don't need to imagine. It's 250 rooms. Basic math," said Valarie. "Okay, Miss Smartypants, now let's go find our room," said Candace. Soon enough, they find their room, which is in the last corner of the floor. The door handle was rusted and full of spider webs.

"Eww! Spider webs! I hate spider webs!" exclaimed Valarie. "Who doesn't hate spider webs?" said Candace. "Well, not me!" said Valarie. They found it hard to open the door as the handle was full of rust. "Finally!" shouted Candace as she jumped straight on the bed. "Are you hungry? I've got some chocolate on me!" said Valarie. "No! I just need to sleep," said Candace.

"More for me! Your loss!" said Valarie. "Fine, give me some," said Candace. They ate some chocolate and went to bed. The tired girls fell asleep immediately, but little did they know what was about to cross their path.

The girls slept peacefully until they heard the door knock. "Can you go get it? I'm tired from driving," said Candace. "Fine," said Valarie as she got up to open the door. "Who was it?" asked Candace. "Well, this is weird. There was no one at the door! I got up for nothing!" said Valarie. A few hours passed by; this time, they heard the doorbell ring. "I'll get it," said Candace. "Thanks," said Valarie.

"I think someone's pranking us! There is no one at the door!" exclaimed Candace. "That's so weird! I didn't even see a doorbell in this room! Can you go check outside?" asked Valarie. "You're right. There is no doorbell. I think we both are daydreaming," said Candace. "More like nightdreaming!" said Valarie. "Good night!" said Candace. "Good night! Hopefully, we won't get disturbed again!" said Valarie.

Soon, they hear the telephone ringing. "don't worry, I'll get it," said Valarie. "Good evening, mam. Would you like some breakfast?" asked Rob. "Oh, it's you. At four in the morning?! Thanks, but no thanks!" said Valarie. "What happened?" asked Candace. "That guy is asking us if we want breakfast! How crazy!" replied Valarie. "Crazy indeed!" said Candace. But then, they heard knocking from the window.

"What was that?!" exclaimed Valarie. "Probably the wind," said Candace. "You're right, I'm being silly," said Valarie. They heard continuous knocking for the next fifteen minutes. But they chose to ignore it. Suddenly, they heard a loud crash! The girls screamed at the top of their lungs! "Help! Help!" they shouted.

They turned on the lights to see a person in a full black suit with a weapon in his hand. The window was broken. The girls ran for their lives. They were afraid of the tiny lift, so they ran down the stairs as fast as they could. "I'm scared!" said Candace. "Keep quiet and run!" said Valarie. They ran and ran till they reached the 3rd floor. They saw a laundry room and decided to hide in it.

They locked the door and slept on top of the washing machines using the clothes as a pillow. "Ow! You are poking me with the room key!" said Candace. "Then you keep it in your pocket!" said Valarie. "Fine!" said Candace as she put the keys in her jacket. "What time is it anyway? My phone is out of charge," said Candace. "It's 6 AM. We should probably get going. Our final is at 12," said Valarie.

They reached the ground floor using the stairs. "Hi there! We're here to check out!" said Valarie. "Sure, girls, did you enjoy your stay here?" asked the new receptionist. "Actually, no. An unfortunate incident happened last night. I have to inform you that an intruder broke open the window of one of your rooms and chased us," said Valarie. "Oh my! That's terrible! Are you girls all right?" she asked.

"We're fine," said Candace. "Do you mind telling me the room number and floor?" asked the receptionist. "Not at all, it's room no. 000 on the fifth floor," answered Valarie. "I'm sorry, but you seem to be mistaken," said the receptionist. "I don't think so?" asked Valarie. "Our room numbers start from 001, not 000." "We don't even have five floors," she said. "That can't be true!" said Candace.

"Go out and see for yourselves!" said the receptionist. The girls went out, only to see that the hotel had only three floors. "Oh my gosh! This is so confusing! We came here yesterday, and a receptionist named Rob let us in and even gave us a key, look!" said Candace while searching for the key. "I'm afraid there is no key," said the receptionist. "Ma'am, yesterday we checked in at this hotel at 2 AM," assured Valarie.

"We went to our room using the lift. Rob even called us to offer breakfast at 4 AM!" said Valarie. "No, dear, this hotel doesn't even provide food," said the receptionist. "No, but then at night, we ran to the laundry room because of the intruder and—" said Valarie. "Oh, girls, I think you both are really tired. There are no receptionists named Rob in this hotel, and I'm the manager!" said the receptionist.

"Did you give Him any money?" she asked. "No, he said that this hotel has a policy that we need to pay only when we check out," replied Valarie. "There is no such thing. Have you ever been to a hotel with that policy? I think you girls had a wild dream. Your stay at our hotel is now free of cost," she said. "Okay then, we better get going!" said Valarie. "I'm so confused!" said Candace.

They got in the car and started to go home. "My Google map is working now, funny, isn't it?" asked Candace. "Yeah, sure is," said Valarie. As she was scrolling through the news, she saw a shocking thing. "Omg, Candace! Look at this! This is the receptionist we saw yesterday! His photo is in the news! It claims that he has gone missing!" exclaimed Valarie. "Omg, even under the same name!

Rob!" said Candace.

The girls reach home, perplexed. They decided to tell Valarie's parents the truth. While her parents heard the story, they smiled and gave a high five to each other.

Maybe it all was just a dream... or was it?

[MORAL: Don't lie. The truth always comes out in the end. Late-night driving is risky. It will make you extremely tired, and at one point, you can't drive properly. Accidents may happen]

CHAPTER 3

THE BABYSITTER

Once, during the summer holidays, Candace was home alone. Candace and Valarie were neighbors and best friends. She was feeling very bored, with no one to play or talk with. So, she decided to take a nap. She was sleeping for hours and hours, but then, she suddenly got a call from Valarie. Wondering what happened, she got up from bed and picked up the call.

"Hi, Candace... um I don't know how to tell you this..." said Valarie. "What happened? Are you all right?" asked Candace. "Yes, I'm fine, but I'm moving to the other side of the earth," said Valarie. "Are you serious right now?! What the" even before Candace could complete her sentence, Valarie interrupted. "I'm sorry, this might be the last time we ever talk to each other. I'm going to change my no. And we sold the house. You should expect ncw neighbors today. Bye," said Valarie.

Candace was dumbstruck. She didn't know what to reply to as this was such a big shock to her. "I wonder what I'm gonna do without her," she thought to herself. Soon enough, she saw moving trucks and a lady going inside her friend's house. "Well, I guess she's gone now. I better go to the neighbor's house, greet them, and welcome them to our neighborhood! I'm going to miss Valarie so bad," she thought.

"Hmm, I can't go empty-handed. Let me whip something up quick," she thought. "What to do, what to do?" "Hmm, maybe cookies! Exactly! Chocolate chip cookies! What's better than moving to a new house and getting cookies from your neighbor?" "Let's see the recipe... butter, sugar, vanilla extract, flour, baking soda, mix!" She put on some music and enjoyed making those cookies.

After an hour, she finally finished making chocolate chip cookies for her new neighbor. She was excited to meet her. She even put a smiley face on the cookies using chocolate glaze. She stepped out of her house to meet the new neighbor. Ding dong! The doorbell rang. A tall woman, wearing a red dress came out of the door. Candace felt that she looked a little odd but shrugged the feeling off her shoulders.

"Hi! I'm your neighbor! Welcome to the neighborhood! I baked you some cookies as a welcome gift!" said Candace. "Oh, how sweet of you, dear! What's your name?" she asked. "My name is Candace. What about you?" asked Candace. "Well, my name is Valarie. Pleased to meet you, dear," said Valarie, the neighbor. "Oh, umm, pleased to meet you too!" replied Candace.

"What happened? Something wrong?" she asked. "Oh no, it's just that my best friend just moved out of this house and had the same name as you!" said Candace. "That's sad. I hope you get to meet your best friend sooner or later!" "I don't think so. She moved to the other side of the earth. But don't worry about that," said Candace. "Okay, dear, I have some packing to do, catch you later!" said 'Valarie'. "Bye!" replied Candace and went on about her day.

She was looking through some old photos of her best friend, wondering where and how she is now. She then watched some TV shows to cheer herself up. After 2 hours or so, she went back to see how the new neighbor was doing. "Hi! How's the moving going?" Candace asked. "Look, I need someone to look after my baby while I'm gone. It's an emergency! I'll give you a hundred bucks. Please do me this favor!" 'Valarie' said.

"100 bucks?! That sure is a lot of money! Hmm, okay! You got yourself a deal! What's her name?" asked Candace. "It's Mellisa, okay, I better get going! The food in the fridge, bye!" said 'Valarie' as she hurriedly rushed out of the house. "Mellisa! Come out, come out wherever you are!" shouted Candace. "Ha! I found you! Come out from there! The place under the table must be dusty!"

"Hi! I'm Mellisa! Who're you?" asked Mellisa. "I'm Candace, and I'm going to babysit you today!" "How are you able to talk so fluently?! You look no older than 1 or 2 years old?!" asked Candace. "Well, I've got my ways! I'm hungry! What ya got?" asked the little girl. "Let me go check the fridge." "Chocolate! Do you want some chocolate?" asked Candace. "Yes, please!" said the little girl, Mellisa.

The girl ate the chocolate and was feeling a little bored, "Oh, I'm feeling so bored! Let's play a game!" she said. "Fine, what game do you want to play?" asked Candace. "That's a tough one... what about hide n' seek?" asked Mellisa. "Sure, why not?" replied Candace. "So, Mellisa, you know how to play the game, right? I'm going to count to ten, then I will try to find you. If I do, I win. If I don't, you win. All right?"

"Agreed," said Mellisa. Candace counted to ten and started to look for Mellisa. After fifteen minutes, she got worried. "Mellisa! You can come out now! You win!" shouted Candace. Suddenly, Mellisa appeared in front of her. Candace let out a blood-curdling scream. "Ahh! How did you do that?! You can disappear?!" shouted Candace.

"Of course, I can. Why? Can't you do that too?" asked the little girl. "No, I cannot. Do that again. I want to see," said Candace. The little girl snapped her fingers and disappeared out of sight. "That's so cool!" said Candace. "Well, if it's cool, then why did you scream?" asked Mellisa. "No reason, I was just startled," answered Candace.

"Let's play another game. What about tag? I'm sure it will be fun!" said Candace. "Sure! I want to start, can I?" asked Mellisa. "Of course you can!" replied Candace. "Tag, you're it!" shouted Mellisa. She ran at the speed of light. Before Candace could blink, she was outside the house. "Oh, I'm too old for this! Come inside, Mellisa. Let's play a game where we can sit," shouted Candace.

"Nah, I'd rather watch TV," Mellisa said. "Okay, whatever suits you!" answered Candace. Time passed by, and after a long time, 'Valarie' returned home, "Oh, finally you're back! Mellisa was such a gem!" said Candace. "Here's your reward! You deserved it!" said 'Valarie'. "Oh, Mellisa! Come out, come out wherever you are!" shouted 'Valarie'. "Bow bow!" said a dog.

"Come here, my cutie pie! Did your neighbor look after you well?" asked 'Valarie'. "What... Mellisa is a dog?" asked Candace in complete shock. "Of course she is! What did you think she was? A wolf? Hahaha," said 'Valarie'. "Umm, yeah, she looked like a wolf... okay, bye! Thanks for the money! Got to get going!" said Candace as she got out of there.

She was so confused; she didn't know what to do. She went to bed, put the money under her pillow, and went to sleep. She woke up due to a call from Valarie. "Hii! What ya up to?" asked Valarie. "Me? What are you doing? How is the shift going? You know, it was so crazy!" said Candace. "I don't know what was so crazy, but the only one crazy is you," said Valarie.

"Well, the new neighbor moved into your house, and you won't believe her name! It's Valarie! I'm going to miss having sleepovers with you!" said Candace. "Why? You can still have sleepovers with me! How does tonight sound? And what's with the moving shifting you're talking about? I'm not going anywhere! This is my hometown!" said Valarie. "But... but... the neighbor had a dog that looked like a wolf named Mellisa and—"

"What has gotten into you? Omg! How did you know?! I got a Siberian husky today and named it Mellisa!" said Valarie. "Oh, I think I'm just having a wild dream... okay,

I'll go freshen up and get ready for tonight's sleepover. Bye!" said Candace. "Well, that was a crazy dream!" she thought to herself. While she was making her bed, she saw 100 bucks under her pillow.

Maybe it all was a dream.... Or was it?

[MORAL: Candace went into a stranger's house just because they offered her money and got into a mess. We should never go into a stranger's house. Even if they are neighbors, you need to get to know them before you do anything of that sort]

THE END